BEING A CHRISTIAN

WHAT BEING A CHRISTIAN IS AND IS NOT

CASEY A FLEET

Casey A Fleet

BEING A CHRISTIAN

WHAT BEING A CHRISTIAN IS AND IS NOT

Casey C Fleet
2002

I Love You!

Cindy... You Rock!

ISBN: 9798677309656

Cover art built in Canva under the Canva free image copyright. 2020 Copyright Canva

About the Author and Dedication photos taken by Bricklyn Tripp

Proofreaders: Raymond Faircloth Jr and Angela Ivey

CONTENTS

Section 1 What being a Christian "is not"

Section 2 What being a Christian "is"

FOREWORD

After having read Rev. Casey Fleet's manuscript entitled, "Being a Christian", (What being a Christian is and is not) I highly recommend it to anyone and all. Christianity goes beyond the decision to accept Christ; it is a lifetime of growing and living out our profession in our everyday lives. The author realizes this and puts it in everyday terminology. We will meet and associate with many people in our walk and many of them will be professing Christians and many will have opinions about how to live and conduct ourselves. The scriptures are our supreme source of strength, knowledge and guide; yet we observe and are told differing opinions as to how to receive the scriptures by any number of people.

As one walks this journey, and indeed the life and walk of a Christian is a journey, we see those 'examples and explanations' of what it is and is not to be a Christian. I believe this book should really be a handbook to be read, not just one time, to remind us indeed of what Christianity "is and is not". Obviously, the scriptures are our guide and yet we need solid accompanying material to assist us and clarify what we claim. Again, "Being a Christian" is just such an assistant in our daily walk.
 Casey uses scriptures abundantly, to stay on track, and I commend him in that regard; he has obviously encountered varying opinions and advice in his Christian walk.

Casey is an ordained minister in the North Carolina Conference of the International Pentecostal Holiness Church and has a definite call to preach on his life. He is actively involved as Youth/Student pastor and in Music ministry and participates in other ministries as well in his home church, "Higher Ground", in Ahoskie NC. He enrolled in the NC Conference School of Ministry (IPHC) in 2012 and has received the three levels of ministry in the IPHC, Local Licensed Minister in 2012, License in 2013 and ordained in 2015; he also received his Associate of Arts in ministry from Holmes Bible College (Greenville, SC) in 2018. Rev. Fleet was also a part of the proofreader team for the Modern English Version of the Bible. He has a continuing desire for knowledge and to grow as a Christian. I have been acquainted with Casey for over nine years and from the beginning of our relationship I have been impressed with his spirit, humility, desire to serve and to grow in Christ. I anxiously anticipate what God will continue to do in his life and ministry.

Rev. Danny Nelson

Superintendent N.C. Conference, IPHC

ACKNOWLEDGEMENTS

First and foremost I acknowledge my Lord and Savior Jesus Christ. Without him my life is incomplete. Without him nothing is possible. Without him I am absolutely nothing. He gets all the honor and glory for all I do.

I want to thank my wife Heather for always being there for me and supporting me in ministry. Through all the ups and downs she is still my biggest supporter.

My daughters Allenah and Kenli Fleet... They are everything to me... It's quite that simple. They are a gift from God!

My parents who raised me and made me the man I am today.

My sister Alyssa for always being a listening ear and trusting me when she needs advice.

My fellow pastors for always being encouragement in times of need. Supporting me always, even when I fall.

My church for love, trust, compassion, and support.

All of Impact Student ministry. Those I have had the privilege of being their youth pastor and to those I will be in the days to come.

Thank you Ray Faircloth Jr. and Angela Ivey for taking the time to proofread this book.

And you! The reader of this book... Thank you!

ENDORSEMENTS

"I can't say enough about this man. I have known him for over 16yrs. Seen the ups and downs of life with him. He is a wonderful husband and father to our two beautiful girls. Hardworking, honorable, noble, just a few attributes of this wonderful man. Since the day of his calling into the ministry, I have seen what God can do in a life if you just allow him too. He has put his all into kingdom work. I could not have asked for a better man to spend my life with. You are truly heaven sent."
Heather Fleet (My beautiful wife)

"For 8+ years Rev. Casey Fleet has been my partner in ministry. When I say this I do not mean it lightly! He's my Best Friend. We've Studied Together, Worked Together, Prayed Together,, Attended School of Ministry Together, Attended Bible College Together! Seriously, even when I was falling behind... He encouraged me to push and finish the course!! I worked very hard and was able to walk across the stage with my brother! This kind of encouragement is what we need more of in ministry! This Pastor is wise beyond his years. As an avid Bible reviewer he has a great deal of knowledge concerning different translations & meanings! I know the heart that he has written this book with! A heart to help you along your journey to draw Closer to the Lord! You will not be disappointed!
Raymond Faircloth Jr. (Higher Ground Church Executive Pastor)

"I've grown up and gone to church and known of Christ and the gospel all of my life. In the time I've known Casey Fleet he has been a fantastic outgoing youth leader, and student of the Bible. He is personally one of my best friends and has taught me many life lessons and has lead me to having a closer relationship with God. So I know this book is going to be a hit and I'm excited to read it."
Johnathan "Jay" Jenkins (Impact Student)

"Pastor Casey Fleet is a workman that need not be ashamed because he has studied and shown himself approved! This anointed man of God is a dedicated Christian, a devoted husband, and an amazing father. His life experiences and challenges are molding him into an incredible example of Godliness. Casey has a very kind demeanor and a passionate worship and preaching style. I love that Casey has an infectious personality, sense of humor and gifting's that that are engaging and essential to the body of Christ. While his target population is the youth; his ministry has a depth that can be understood by everyone. It has been my honor to co-pastor with this man of valor for many years and my esteemed joy to be his friend."
Angel Sease (Higher Ground Church Associate Pastor)

"I have known Casey for the majority of my life. He is an incredible teacher, pastor, and friend. I grew up in church and I have known Christ my entire life. From time to time I have questioned many things and Casey was always there to answer. He has made a huge impact on my life and has drew me closer to God. The lessons taught every Wednesday night have stuck with me and I apply them to every situation in my life. I know for a fact this book will impact every individual who reads it. I hope it teaches and inspires people just like how it inspired me."
Alyssa Miller (Impact Student)

"Casey Fleet is a rare individual. He is a devoted family man, an amazing youth pastor and one the best audio/visual techs I've met. Casey loves life, laughs harder than most and is always looking for the fun in any situation. He also loves God wholeheartedly, and serves Him passionately. He is an avid student of the Word and an excellent example of a true worshiper. He is also my friend, and I consider it an honor to write this endorsement for his first book. I know that it's contents will bless you as much as just knowing Casey has blessed me."
Rich Burkett (Impact College Pastor)

"I have known Casey for a good portion of my life. He is not only an extremely anointed pastor, but a great friend, and mentor to many. He and his family have been a true blessing in my life. I'm grateful for all of endless support he has shown me as well as each and everyone of his teens. He has taught me many life lessons, and I'm excited and proud to be apart of this next chapter in his life.
Bricklyn Tripp (Impact Student)

"Pastor Casey Fleet is a man I call friend and colleague. I have seen him in hard times and in good times, yet never seen him lose faith in God. As I look at him growing in faith I am astonished at the knowledge that he has of the word of God which only comes by studying the word and being a steward of that word. Casey it is an honor to call you friend and pastor. I look forward to what God has in store in the years to come."
Robert Knox (Higher Ground Church Associate pastor)

PREFACE

Being a Christian is a small simple book to provide some basic truths about Christianity. We live in a world where Christians are held to the highest standard yet looked down upon at the same time. This book is not extensive and it is not theologically deep. It is not driven by any doctrinal agendas. It's simply to help you in your sharing of your Faith. Sometimes it helps to know how to address people with the basic areas of our walk.

The idea of this book came to me one day during a Facebook post. In the midst of a crazy year (2020)... I feel as if God is purging Christianity of the unnecessary. And in the midst of this we need to be strong in our faith by remembering who we are and who we are not.

I believe you are reading this by divine appointment and that God will use you through this book.

I love you and hope you enjoy this book.

Casey Fleet

INTRODUCTION

Introduction by my Pastor Ray Faircloth Sr.

It's an honor to share my thoughts in Pastor Casey Fleets first of what I believe will be many books. I have seen him grow in the grace and knowledge of the Lord Jesus Christ as he has passionately dedicated himself to study and prayer. The Higher Ground Church family of Ahoskie, NC has witnessed the calling and progression on Pastor Casey from the actual start up in ministry to him becoming a dynamic communicator of the Gospel to youth and adults alike.

Casey is indeed a true Youth Pastor who has been anointed and appointed with the incredible assignment of reaching young people "where they are and as they are" in Northeastern North Carolina. By my own past experiences I know and can personally attest to the fact that youth pastoring is not easy or for the faint hearted. Remaining youthfully minded does not always set well with others, especially other adults.

No, It's not an easy assignment, however... as Higher Ground Church' lead pastor I can sincerely say that Pastor Casey's Church family has had his back and stood with him in good times and a few not so good times, and without a doubt, the Higher Ground Church family sincerely appreciates his passion and leadership. The church continues to rejoice over his success in sowing biblical truths and moral principles deeply into the lives of young men and women in the community.

Before I change gears, let me say one more thing about my friend and son in the faith, Casey Fleet,

Youth pastor is only one of many responsibilities that falls on his shoulders. He and his lovely wife Heather oversee our Children's

Ministry. He is effectively engaged in managing the communications ministry of the church which required a complete overhaul in 2020 to accommodate the COVID-19 crisis and social distancing expectations. We are grateful for Gods continual calling and anointing on his life.

As a pastor, I take very serious the question regarding being a Christian or what is a Christian. The question is actually so simple that many scholars and theologians trip over it, causing earnest and sincere seekers to lose their way on the road to redemption. According to Proverbs 13:15, "The way of the transgressor is hard", so if the way of the sinner is hard, I would think in contrast, the way of the righteous is not hard or at least not as hard.

In fact, Jesus said to come to me, for "my yoke is easy and my burden is light" (Matthew 11:30). Sadly man has made the experience of salvation so very hard and sometimes unreachable.

From the beginning, when "THE WORD" became flesh, when "JESUS", (God in the flesh) was first revealed, from then, until now, Ministers and Ministries have complicating the simple message of Salvation and Redemption with a twisted legalistic clothesline of rules and regulations that has ultimately choked the spiritual life out of many innocent new born babes in Christ.

Dear friend, if you are one of the millions who have turned aside and walked away from proclaiming your relationship and liberty in Christ because of the expectations of others, I sincerely plead with you to Return to a Church in your community. There's a church near you that's in the business of rescuing and restoring the spiritually wounded.

In fact, I truly believe that God is raising up Churches, Leaders and Pastors who are driven by a dream to rescue the perishing and restore those how have fallen or tripped along the way.

I'm reminded of a wonderful Old Testament passage from Micah 7:8 " Rejoice not against me O my enemy! For when I have fallen, I shall arise."

That means you my friend. You can get up with the proclamation.

"At last At Last, my past is past."

You were not born for failure.., you were born to successfully serve the Lord and be a witness of his redeeming Grace.

In conclusion, I submit, a Christian is someone who has accepted Jesus Christ as their LORD and Savior. Someone with complete trust and a dialog on a daily basis with this same LORD and CHRIST.

Our salvation and complete trust in the LORD JESUS CHRIST is demonstrated by our reliance on his teachings. "He who hears and will do these sayings of mine". Find out what he said; Matthew, chapters 5,6 and 7 and follow his guidance.

Christ even made the teachings of the Commandments so simple that two commandments under his guidance would actually keep you on track in obedience to the will of God the Father. Matthew 22:37-40 "Love the LORD THY GOD with all of your heart, your soul and your mind, and Love your neighbor as yourself. On these two commandments hang all the laws of the past and future prophets" (RFF Translation)

The Commandments dealing with God are Vertical (He's the LORD of ALL or He's not Lord at all). The Commandments dealing with others (our neighbors) are Horizontal.

You can't knowingly mistreat your parents, your spouse or others and be comfortable as a CHRISTIAN.

However, (and this may be my most important statement), Conviction and dialog with God will always bring us back to the place of Grace and forgiveness which He graciously offers. So, there you have it in it's simplicity from my perspective. As simple as it sounds, LOVE GOD and LOVE YOUR NEIGHBOR!!

That's what Christians Do!

By The Way; If you truly Love God, you won't be putting other god's before Him, which includes Emmanuel (God With Us).

If you truly Love God, You won't be taking His precious name in vain, and you'll highly prioritize your time during the week to assemble in His house with other believers. If you truly love others as commanded in the sayings of Christ you will not steal their belongings nor will you lie or bare false witness.

That second part about others includes dishonoring or disrespecting parents. A true salvation relationship with Christ Jesus will cause you to honor your Father and Mother.

It's been an incredible journey to boldly proclaim my faith in Christ as a Christian for over fifty years, with a calling on my life to Preach the Gospel since I was 15 years old. Throughout the years there have been many ups and downs, but because of the magnificent grace and true simplicity of the Gospel..... there has been NO... IN and OUTS.

Thank God I know that I know that I know........ I'm Saved!

And you are too Christian friend, if you've surrendered your life and sold out to him as your LORD GOD, Master and Savior.

- Pastor Ray Faircloth Sr., D.Min

SECTION 1

WHAT BEING A CHRISTIAN CHRISTIAN

"IS NOT"

CHAPTER 1

IS NOT EASY

"Then Jesus told his disciples, "If anyone would come after me, let him deny himself and take up his cross and follow me. For whoever would save his life will lose it, but whoever loses his life for my sake will find it." Matthew 16:24-25 ESV

Being a Christian is not easy. In echoing the words of Jesus when he told his disciples to deny themselves and take up their cross. He didn't stop there when he said in order to save your life you must lose it, but whenever you lose your life for his name sake you will find it. Jesus was simply saying to his disciples that being a Christian is not easy. If you were going to follow me, you have a tough road ahead. The implications of taking up our cross and denying our self are far deeper than just a heavy cross on our back. In fact, the implications at times can be a life full of trials, temptations, hardships, valleys, and even tribulations or persecution. That echoes even truer today as Christianity is one of the most hated and persecuted religions on earth. There are many different articles and books that share this alarming information.

In verse twenty six of Matthew chapter sixteen Jesus asked his disciples a very profound question... He said, "what would it benefit you to gain the whole world and lose your soul?" Jesus was basically saying this world offers an easy way out and you have the option to take it the easy way or the "not so easy" way. Being a Christian is not always easy because sometimes we must shun the things of this world. Often in doing so the world looks down on us for not having the same mind and or spirit.

Another reason being a Christian is not always easy is because when God tells us not to do something and we do it anyway it is a sin. Likewise, when God tells us to do something and we do not do it we are sinning as well. It's kind of one of those vice versa moments that hits me hard sometimes even as a leader. There are a plethora of things that God has asked us to do as Christians and many times we fail to do so (including me). Things like love God and your neighbor (everyone), don't forsake the assembling of yourselves together (church), go and preach the gospel to all the world, give to the poor, pay tithes, spend more time in worship to God, do not boast, do not over eat (I fail big time), take care of widows, etc. etc. The list could go on and on and be tough to meet the requirements. In fact it's nearly impossible for us to reach the requirements. Many times these requirements are to show us the holiness of God and the unrighteousness of man.

It should also be said that being a Christian is not easy because it is a risk or chance taken. One of the toughest aspects of my life about claiming Jesus Christ is the fact that not everyone I know is a Christian. Not everyone that I associate with on a daily basis is a Christian. I also have many friends that I grew up with that are not Christian, and although I love them and would do anything for them at the drop of a hat there's a good chance that they would not do the same for me. Talk about not easy! I mean, we really do not feel or think as if we are better than someone else. In the minds of others and their lack of understanding our faith it seems that way. I have literally laid in bed many nights praying and thinking about people that I know that do not know Christ. Countless sleepless nights thinking about their lives and their souls. Not easy!

Going back to the passage in Matthew chapter 16 probably the biggest implication of this passage of taking up our cross is the fact that it could mean death. In an absolute worst-case scenario for Christians is we face the possibility of death just for being Christians. Now I know this is not as common in American Christianity, but it is very common in other countries throughout the world, especially Third World countries. In fact, here in America we have a plethora of English Bible translations that we can choose from, yet in other countries they do not even have the Bible in their language. I'm so spoiled to my Bible that I can't even imagine going one day without reading scripture.

I was sitting in a class and the speaker was telling us a story about someone he knew that went to a Third World country to do some ministry work. It is a story that will stick with me the rest of my life. I do not remember the full details of the story, but I do remember the importance of the story. He said when he got to the country or the area, he was to go introduce himself to a specific person, and then that person took him and dropped him off to meet another person, and then that person took him and dropped him off to yet another person. This happened three times before they went to where they were going. When he met this third person, he was taken down an alleyway and told to be very very quiet in fact don't even speak. They come to a door and the guy says something in another language so that the people inside would open the door. He said when they went in it was a bunch of people standing around very very quietly. The people had tears coming from their eyes as they were passing around one page that they had from the New Testament in their language. They were so overwhelmed with what they were reading. He said they would make a clapping motion without their hands touching so they could be very quiet. It's quite clear that he was part of an underground church. These Christians had to be very quiet because if they got caught, they could be thrown into prison or even killed. This story has always been very thought-provoking for me because it is a reminder that just because Christianity can be easy for some of us at times, it is very daunting and dangerous for others of our faith.

Lastly being a Christian is not easy because it was not easy for Jesus. He came into this world knowing the task at hand... To save humanity! Can you imagine that burden? In a world that is full of hate anger and division, your job is to save it. Not only is your job to save it, but by being betrayed by that world. In Isaiah chapter fifty three we see many things that Jesus would (and did) face.

"He is despised and rejected by men, A Man of sorrows and acquainted with grief. And we hid, as it were, our faces from Him; He was despised, and we did not esteem Him. Surely He has borne our griefs And carried our sorrows; Yet we esteemed Him stricken, Smitten by God, and afflicted. But He was wounded for our transgressions, He was bruised for our iniquities; The chastisement for our peace was upon Him, And by His stripes we are healed. All we like sheep have gone astray; We have turned, every one, to his own way; And the LORD has laid on Him the iniquity of us all. He was oppressed and He was afflicted, Yet He opened not His mouth; He was led as a lamb to the slaughter, And as a sheep before its shearers is silent, So He opened not His mouth. He was taken from prison and from judgment, And who will declare His generation? For He was cut off from the land of the living; For the transgressions of My people He was stricken. And they made His grave with the wicked— But with the rich at His death, Because He had done no violence, Nor was any deceit in His mouth."
Isaiah 53:3-9 NKJV

Despised, rejected, suffered, took up our pain, bore our suffering, punished by God, stricken, afflicted, wounded, crushed, punished, oppressed, cut off, and killed. Talk about going through some not so easy times. So as Christians we must always keep in mind that although Christianity is not always easy; our Lord Jesus Christ knows the pain. It was not easy for Him, yet he did it for you and for me.

Being a Christian is not easy, but the rewards far exceed the risks.

CHAPTER 2

IS NOT FUN

"choosing rather to be mistreated with the people of God than to enjoy the fleeting pleasures of sin."
Hebrews 11:25 ESV

Being a Christian is not fun. At the beginning of Hebrews chapter 11 we see the explanation of what faith is. Then as the chapter goes on, we see how God's children throughout history have operated through faith. The chapter mentions people like Abel, Enoch, Noah, Abraham, Sarah, Jacob, Joseph, and then there's Moses. When Moses had grown up he refused to be called the son of Pharaoh's daughter. Separating himself from the treasures of Egypt. Rather than him enjoying the pleasures of life and sin he chose to be afflicted. It would have been much easier for him to "live it up" and enjoy sinful life. Yet his choice was to separate himself from the things of this world.

So why in the world would I say being a Christian is not fun, yet I enjoy being a Christian so much?

The answer falls within the understanding of what I mean by "fun". When I speak of "fun" I am referencing the things we are tempted to engage in that are willful sin. Because let's face it, sin is fun. That's why we do it and it's so easy. This is not to say Christians don't or can't have fun. I can assure you that I am a prime example of someone that can have good clean Christian fun and not care what anyone thinks. I mean I do have a rapper alias that is "lil pickle" (don't ask me what started that). I have also been known to make some of the more religious folk cringe by being a huge jokester sometimes more than they think I should. But it is saying we have to refrain from the things of this world. At the end of the day being a Christian absolutely rocks! Especially when you get to go to youth hangouts, revivals, mission trips, worship services, conferences, camps, and all the other fun stuff we get to do, and although we have those things as Christians, the world has a "fun" to offer as well. We are not to engage in these activities it can feel as if we are left out or not having fun as Christians.

As a youth pastor I have ministered to many students both preteen and post teen that have struggled with this very issue. They want so bad to be close to God and at the same time be close to their friends that are not close to God. Oh, and by the way I have ministered to many adults that have struggled with the same struggles. So this isn't just something that plagues young people. It plagues all people at some point in their lives, and when it does, it is not fun. When I get text messages and phone calls from my students wanting to know what they should do because they have been asked to go do something they shouldn't, it isn't easy to navigate. Explaining that sometimes saying "no" to people you consider your friends is not fun or easy to do. You have to sit back and watch them have all the fun while you sit alone in the midst of your mixed emotions and feelings. It is a struggle I know all too well. Even sometimes those you say "no" to end up drifting from you and your friendship deteriorates and makes you want to compromise.

There may be times when you make the mistake of compromise just for the sake of fun or friendship. This makes all the matters worst for a few reasons. The first reason is you have let down God, and when we as Christians know we let down our Father for the sake of sin it hurts us and him. Secondly we can tarnish our testimony to others. Have you ever heard someone say, "I can't believe they did that; they are supposed to be Christian"... ? So, when we compromise for worldly fun as Christians the same "world" is the first to watch the way we live, and when we do this it lets down God yet again. Lastly you let down yourself. This can be dangerous because I have seen people make these mistakes enough, they begin to think they are not worthy of God's grace. These types of let downs can lead to the downward spiral of anxiety and depression.

I have had many occasions in my life on both sides of this fence. I lived my life as a teenager giving in to the "fun" of the world. Drinking, Drugs, and premarital sex were all things I thought were fun. Little did I know these things would have lasting effects on my life. Many years later I have apologized to people for things that I did in the name of "fun". All of which happened when I placed the things of the world over my relationship with God. Now that I have a relationship with God, I understand how blessed I was to make through these times. I have had some of the same opportunities as a Christian and have turned them down with ease. I have been able to sit with friends in motorcycle clubs drinking and not drink a drop, sit with people cussing and not say a word, listen to stories of adultery and stay pure, and many other things that happen when we become adults.

"Now the serpent was more crafty than any other beast of the field that the Lord God had made. He said to the woman, "Did God actually say, 'You shall not eat of any tree in the garden'?"
Genesis 3:1 ESV

In Genesis chapter 3 verse one there are a couple things to look at. The first being how the enemy came as a serpent. At this time, the serpent was just another animal created by God, and was not viewed as bad but good. Because remember all things that God had created were good. The second thing to take notice of here is that he was crafty. Even more so than any of the other beast of the field. So this means the enemy came as if he was something good with a crafty divisive scheme for us to sin. To put it in layman's terms, he made sin look fun, and he was successful in doing so because both Eve and

Adam fell for it. But not without repercussion. Later in the same chapter we see that God punishes Satan, Eve, and Adam for their rebellion. So, what started out looking good and seeming to be fun ended up with punishment. A lasting punishment that we are still experiencing today.

It would be so easy for all of us to just give up and give in. But remember this... Christianity is not something we follow for fun. We don't follow Christ because it is some kind of game. It is a war we are in. We are fighting a spiritual battle that the world does not understand. It can be tough at times. It can be "not so fun"... But I encourage you to keep doing right and keep doing all you do for the glory of God.

CHAPTER 3

IS NOT PERFECTION

"for all have sinned and fall short of the glory of God,"
Romans 3:23 ESV

Being a Christian is not perfection. I love how the apostle Paul addresses the church in Romans chapter 3. Especially earlier in the chapter from verse 10 onward when he talks about how there is no one righteous, not even one! This chapter has always been a reminder to me that I am not perfect. Especially as long as I wear a robe of flesh.

Now in technical terms Christians are actually perfect in Christ. However, we must understand that it's a spiritual perfection. While we carry a spiritual perfection, we also carry imperfection in flesh.

Yes... We too mess up!!!

This... Oh the irony of all the misconceptions of Christians and who we are supposed to be. This one could be the icing on the cake. In fact, I could probably write an entire book on this simple misconception. A world that holds us to a standard of perfection, we hold each other to a standard of perfection, all the while we wear a robe of flesh. Destined to make a mistake and slip up somewhere, somehow at some point. Boy oh boy when we do... Here comes those watching and waiting to devour us. Hypocrites, Christians are hypocrites. I have heard this many times in my life. There have even been some to say things like "some kind of pastor you are"... As if I am always supposed to say and do the right things. Sometimes what you say or do may not even be wrong or sinful, but in opposition to someone's opinions. I love the quote that says something along the lines of "I'd rather go to church with hypocrites than to go to hell with them". In all honesty it's the truth. I go to church with messed up people. I myself have and have had many struggles. Church is where we go to edify, build up, love, disciple, and deploy. It's not a place for finger pointing, discord, and division.

"The perfect place, for imperfect people"
Higher Ground Church[1]

The perfect place for imperfect people is the motto you will see when you walk into the doors of Higher Ground Church in Ahoskie North Carolina. It is a saying that should be true for all churches. As pastor Ray Faircloth Sr states many times in his teaching and preaching:

---

[1] www.ahoskie.us

"There are no perfect people in this place... If you are perfect you may want to leave because you will mess us up. There are no halos in this house"
Pastor Ray Faircloth Sr.

As Christians we do not promote sin. In fact we do promote a life of Holiness as a standard. However, we must understand that pure Holiness and imperfection is only of God. One of my own personal quotes is "Holiness is no perfection, it's the pursuit of perfection". Understanding we in the "flesh" and can't be perfect, we must understand the pursuit is what's perfect. God is holy, I am not! It's quite that simple... However, I can live a life of purity and holiness simply by what I chase after in this life. If you are in hot pursuit of Jesus, his way of thinking, his way of living, and his righteousness... That's what makes you holy. Jesus is your righteousness. Jesus is your holiness. Jesus is your perfection. Jesus is your eternity. Jesus is your love. Jesus is your hope. Jesus is your everything. Jesus is... Not you! Not me!

Then you have to deal with those that "think" as if they are perfect... Shake my head... The ones that are self-righteous. You know what I am talking about. Those in the church that are definitely Pharisees through and through. They are so much better than everyone else in all they say, think, and do. The ones that will cut you down for anything and everything, even if it was not sin. You have to walk on eggshells all the time because you are afraid, they will get mad over something small and silly. I have been attacked by these "perfect" people so many times in my ministry. Can't even have good clean fun without them coming at you sometimes. Let's not forget the King James Bible is the only true word of God[2]... lol... (It's really not) Okay Okay...

What about Matthew 5:48? Didn't Jesus clearly command us to be perfect?

> "Therefore you shall be perfect, just as your Father in heaven is perfect."
> Matthew 5:48 NKJV

This is one of many "scripture bomb" verses. A scripture bomb verse is when people use scripture to try and prove a point. Many times, it is done outside of context. There is nothing wrong with using scripture to prove a point. In fact, I use them in this book throughout to prove points. When scripture does not correctly fit the narrative, but is used like it does is when it becomes a scripture bomb. It is very important that we read passages before and after these "Bombs" so we can fully understand what is being said. Kind of like the "judge not" verse that everyone wants to use when you say something is wrong... (SMH).

Here in Matthew 5 Jesus clearly says, "be perfect", so how can I write a chapter on Being a Christian is "not perfection"?

---

[2] It's really not but there are really people who believe it is and you are sinning for not using it. I love KJV... Just not as much as some do.

If you back up a little in this passage you get this:

"You have heard that it was said, 'You shall love your neighbor and hate your enemy.' But I say to you, love your enemies, bless those who curse you, do good to those who hate you, and pray for those who spitefully use you and persecute you, that you may be sons of your Father in heaven; for He makes His sun rise on the evil and on the good, and sends rain on the just and on the unjust. For if you love those who love you, what reward have you? Do not even the tax collectors do the same? If you greet your brethren only, what do you do more than others? Do not even the tax collectors do so? Therefore you shall be perfect, just as your Father in heaven is perfect."
Matthew 5:43-48 NKJV

Jesus is talking clearly about love in this passage. Not just love, but love towards those who are our enemies. A love so deep we are willing to even bless those who come against us. A love so deep we will pray for those that persecute us. Remember this persecution isn't someone simply lying on us. This isn't your typical Western world persecution. This is third world persecution. A persecution that could end in death. Can you image with a sincere heart literally praying for someone as they were getting ready to murder you? Jesus did and so should we. As hard as it may sound. In fact if we only love those who love us what good is it really? When we show love to those people that absolutely hate us is when the perfect love of God radiates. It's not our perfect love, but the perfect love of God. This is what Jesus meant by be perfect as your Father in heaven. It is to radiate a perfect love in situations you normally can't. Jesus didn't mean you lose perfection by making mistakes in life.

For clarity knowing we are not righteous and perfect without Christ does NOT mean we can do as we wish and use the imperfection card. Even the Apostle Paul made it clear when he said we should not continue to sin just because grace abounds. Continuous willful sin is wrong on all levels. But thank God we have grace, mercy, and forgiveness to get us through. We are not perfect but we serve a perfect God. Our only perfection is in him and him alone.

CHAPTER 4

IS NOT A CLUB

"For the grace of God has appeared, bringing salvation for all people," Titus 2:11 ESV

Being a Christian is not a club. The scripture is quite clear all throughout that Jesus came to bring salvation to all men. Christianity is not a club just for the elect or the privileged. Churches are not clubhouses for racism, seclusion, private meetings, or scheming. In fact, if there are churches (and I'm sure there are) that deal in such things they are more less a cult. Christianity is an open invitation to all people from God, not from man. It's not up to us to pick and choose who are to be in God's kingdom, and not only that but there are no membership fees, there are no dues to be paid. Because Jesus paid our dues and paid our fees some 2000 years ago on the cross.

In this short chapter I'm going to try and give you a few differences between the church and a club. When I say club I am referencing like a country club, a club that you have to be a member of before you can belong to it by paying some sort of due our fee.

Become before belong

In most all club memberships you have to pay some sort of fee or due before you can be a part. In most cases, you have to pay some sort of due or fee before you can even enter. In the region I live there is a place that you can become a member of called Colerain Beach. I'm not so sure if it's still a membership entrance... But I do know it used to be. All it is is a beach on the river with a pavilion and I do believe it has restrooms and changing rooms. It's nice and even has a peer. I think I have been there maybe a couple of times since I've lived here, and the only way that I could go is if a member took me. Memberships like this are created to not only fund clubs, but to protect the club from outsiders. There's nothing wrong with this. However, the church is not a club. You do not need some sort of paid membership before you can enter, you do not need another member to let you in, there is not a gated community or guard house, and there is no partiality.

Now, I do understand the term "belong before you believe" can be tricky to some. I do not believe a church membership can get you into heaven. But for the sake of this book I do need to give clarity that when I say belong before you believe I'm referencing outsiders coming to the church. Not becoming the church. It's more of a statement that you are welcome here even before you know what being a Christian is all about. It's more of a statement showing we have nothing to hide as Christians.

What goes on within the four walls of our buildings it's not that of a secret society. You are welcome here!

Ultimately what will happen is people who come before they believe will either end up believing or end up leaving. It will be up to them to make the choice to be part of the kingdom of God.

For us by us

Unlike country clubs and membership club programs... The church is not a "for us by us" entity. The church was created by God for God. It is a place where believers come together to receive learning, wisdom, edification, and insight. It's where we gather to worship a sovereign God and gain strength so that when we leave, we can take the gospel to the world. So, if we want to be completely technical the church is more so for God and for the world. Because it's God's design to use the church as an army that can bring more to the church.

There is a huge issue and misconception today as to what the church is and what the church is for. Too many times people look at the church as if it's something for us by us. People go to church only to seek what they can get out of it, instead of what they can put in. So, in this I do have to address that there are people that go to church that are Christian and non-Christian that do view the church as if it is some sort of club. The whole purpose of this chapter is to remind everyone that the church is not a clubhouse.

Yes, you can come before you belong, yes, it is a place that has open doors to all people. In this you must know that it is in hopes of winning a soul to Jesus Christ. It's not about another tither... It's not about stacking numbers... It's not about young people or old people. It's about ALL people and the fact that God's desire is for ALL people to come to know him.

> "For this is good and acceptable in the sight of God our Savior, who desires all men to be saved and to come to the knowledge of the truth."
> I Timothy 2:3-4 NKJV

Paul tells Timothy here that it is God's desire that all men[3] be saved and come to the knowledge of truth. This is why as Christians we must understand that our churches are not clubhouses. They are places that we need to be inviting people to, no matter who they are or where they're from. Rich or Poor, Black or White, Man or Woman, it doesn't matter. In hopes that they can come to the knowledge of truth, and by doing so we are helping fulfill God's desire. Paul and his letter to Timothy was not the only one to make this claim. Peter also made the same claim when he said this:

---

[3] people

"The Lord is not slow to fulfill his promise as some count slowness, but is patient toward you, not wishing that any should perish, but that all should reach repentance."
2 Peter 3:9 ESV

My earnest prayer is that the church is a place where all feel welcome. No matter what they bring or don't bring they should be able to come. My heart is to see men and women, boys and girls, whites and black, rich and poor all coming together in worship not feeling the pressure of placement. Yes, sinners are welcome... Yes, they may or may not be changed. This does NOT mean we compromise the Gospel of Jesus Christ. We preach truth in love the sinner may come to repentance. This cannot happen if we treat Christianity as a whole as if it is a club for us by us.

It is a crying shame that people have to worry about walking into the doors of a church and being judged because of what they wear, what they have done, the color of their skin, or their bank account status. There are churches all over this country that will all but shun you if you don't wear a suit and dress. Be careful to make sure your shirt is tucked in. I will never forget going to fill in preaching at a church one time and one of the deacons come up to me before I was going to preach and asked me if I would tuck in my shirt. The particular shirt I was wearing was actually not made to be tucked in. However, humbly out of compliance I went and tucked my shirt in. But I can assure you I did not preach there a next time. I have also been to churches where all the women are to never cut their hair and to always wear dresses. Now if that's their personal conviction it's fine. But if a person comes there that is an outsider or not a Christian, they should not feel shunned for not following suit. We all know Christianity is not about what you wear, it's not about the color of your skin, it's not about how much money you have. It's simply about your relationship with Jesus Christ. Church is not a club it is a hospital for all who are sick. Church is a docking station for the child of God to recharge and refuel.

"Come to me, all you who are weary and burdened, and I will give you rest."
Matthew 11:28 NIV

CHAPTER 5

IS NOT DEAD

"It shall come to pass in the latter days that the mountain of the house of the Lord shall be established as the highest of the mountains, and shall be lifted up above the hills; and all the nations shall flow to it, and many peoples shall come, and say: "Come, let us go up to the mountain of the Lord, to the house of the God of Jacob, that he may teach us his ways and that we may walk in his paths." For out of Zion shall go forth the law, and the word of the Lord from Jerusalem."
Isaiah 2:2-3 ESV

Being a Christian is not dead. Many may think that being a Christian is not the "thing" anymore. They may think that due to the standards of righteous living people just don't want to follow. But I can tell you from personal experience this is far from the truth. People are seeking something more. People are seeking to fill that void in their lives. People are seeking truth! Therefore

Christianity and or being a Christian is not dead, is not dying, and certainly is not outdated.

I honestly believe that as the world gets worse and worse, we will see more people seek spiritual truth and fulfillment. The reason the world is so evil is simply because people seek fulfillment from the things of this world. The things of this world are only momentary. They will not and cannot last. They only provide temporary fulfillment that leaves you "high and dry".

"Do not lay up for yourselves treasures on earth, where moth and rust destroy and where thieves break in and steal, but lay up for yourselves treasures in heaven, where neither moth nor rust destroys and where thieves do not break in and steal. For where your treasure is, there your heart will be also."
Matthew 6:19-21 ESV

Talk about things that are momentary. Jesus told us thieves would take what we have here and if the thieves don't take it natural occurrence of decay will take it. So what Jesus is telling us is that absolutely nothing in the physical will last long. You may enjoy the things of this world for a little while but eventually they'll turn on you. Eventually they will be dated and no good. Eventually they will become old. I remember a couple of years ago I was teaching my youth a series of lessons coming into the Christmas season. In fact, I probably started around Thanksgiving teaching being thankful. I remember asking them what they were getting for Christmas and some of what they were hoping to get. They were all extremely excited about the new things that were coming their way. New phone, Xbox, PlayStation, AirPods, iPads, computers, clothes, money, and all sorts of other super awesome stuff. Oh, the glory of something NEW! But then I asked them what's wrong with their phones, games, clothes, and all the same stuff they already had... and pretty much universally the answers were all similar... These things are getting old, or I want the new product. So, I used this opportunity to remind them that no matter how something new is, and no matter how nice it is. One day it will get old to you and you will want a renewal. You will be seeking for something more. We are always looking for renewed fulfillment when it comes to the things of this world.

So why is this important and what does it have to do with Christianity not being dead?

Considering the fact people are always in search of fulfillment, there will always be a "hole" or void in the heart of all people. The only way to fill that void is with something that can be placed there that will not decay. Something that will not get stolen, something that will not get old. Guess what the only solution is... It's Jesus Christ. He not only gives us hope in this world but in the world to come. He proves eternal hopes that no man can take away from us. Christian lifestyle is not dead because we can walk in joy and peace knowing our happiness is not based upon what we face in the present. Our happiness is set on heavenly things that we already know have a glory beyond our comprehension.

Christianity is not dead because God certainly is not dead. He is alive and well. He is the daily renewal of life. He provides us all the grace to live another day. He provides us all a mercy, love, and grace to be in his presence at all times. We, all of us Christian or not have never known a moment outside of the care and presence of a Sovereign God. The more people seek truth, the more they will find Christ. Jesus has made a way for us all to fill every void in our lives by giving us hope.

Christianity is not dead because Christ is the only way. He is the only way to fill the void in the now and for the future. He is the only way to live temporary and he is the only way to live eternal. "Jesus said to him, "I am the way, the truth, and the life. No one comes to the Father except through Me." (John 14:6 NKJV). There is no other way for us to enter into the presence of a Holy God. Jesus is our key to the Kingdom. He is our entrance into the door. Jesus said I am life, and he meant not only life as we live it but life eternal. Jesus is telling us that not only is Christianity not dead, but it is needed. It is needed for all people to have eternal life. It would be our mission and goal to show a world that not only is our movement alive and well. But it is our movement and only our movement that provides true comfort and peace in place of the void. It is our movement that stops one from seeking the "new" of the spiritual world.

Christianity is not dead because we are justified by faith alone. "For by grace you have been saved through faith, and that not of yourselves; it is the gift of God, not of works, lest anyone should boast." (Ephesians 2:8-9 NKJV). Saved solely by God's loving caring and unending grace that gives us the ability to believe in him. We are not saved by what we do or what we say. We are justified by our faith in Jesus. Other world religions have prerequisites for salvation. Most all of them have a salvation system that is based upon works. Some of them the more you do the easier to "get in", or the more you do the easier to "stay in". The danger in such is the provision for boasting. "I did this" and "I did that"... The truth is our merits and righteousness are absolutely nothing in the face of a Holy God. In Christianity we have a realization that we can not save ourselves and thank God for that because if salvation was truly based upon our works, we are all doomed.

In the Lifeway "facts and trends" article by Aaron Earls written June 11, 2019[4]: "Globally, Christianity is growing at a 1.27% rate. Currently, there are 2.5 billion Christians in the world. The world's population, 7.7 billion, is growing at a 1.20% rate. Islam (1.95%), Sikhs (1.66%) and Hindus (1.30%) are the only religious groups growing faster than Christianity, though followers of Jesus outnumber every other faith and are predicted to continue to do so at least

---

[4] https://factsandtrends.net/2019/06/11/7-surprising-trends-in-global-christianity-in-2019/

through 2050." These statistics came from "The status of global Christianity" by the center for the Study of Global Christianity[5] at Gordon-Conwell Theological Seminary.

So according to these statistics Christianity is not dead nor close to it. At one of our slowest growth rates in history we will still be the largest religion in the world even past 2050. As the world continues the deteriorate, I do believe that our rates will go higher. In fact other statistics to show in some countries our rates much higher. I say all that to say this... We are not alone! Our God is alive and well! Our mission and commission need to be one of reaching a world trying to fill a void. Let's do this... Christianity is not dead and will not die. Not only is Christianity "not" dead but neither are the followers of the movement. We are seeing a growing trend of Christians take a strong stand for truth that sets the captive free.

Christianity can't be dead... The tomb is empty!

Not only is the tomb empty but it was seen empty, not just told. It was not rumor or word of mouth. Jesus was seen in his resurrected body by the disciples after leaving the tomb.

He is alive! So are we!

---

[5] https://www.gordonconwell.edu/wp-content/uploads/sites/13/2019/04/StatusofGlobalChristianity20191.pdf

"Now after the Sabbath, as the first day of the week began to dawn, Mary Magdalene and the other Mary came to see the tomb. Behold, there was a great earthquake; for an angel of the Lord descended from heaven, and came and rolled back the stone from the door, and sat on it. His countenance was like lightning, and his clothing as white as snow. The guards shook for fear of him, and became like dead men. But the angel answered and said to the women, "Do not be afraid, for I know that you seek Jesus who was crucified. He is not here; for He is risen, as He said. Come, see the place where the Lord lay. Go quickly and tell His disciples that He is risen from the dead, and indeed He is going before you into Galilee; there you will see Him. Behold, I have told you.""
Matthew 28:1-7 NKJV

Now go quickly and tell everyone!!! Jesus is not dead!!! He is alive!!!

CHAPTER 6

IS NOT SELF FULFILLMENT

"He must increase, but I must decrease."" John 3:30 ESV

Being a Christian is not self-fulfillment. Better yet it is more so self-denial. Many people come or seek Christianity for what they can get out of it rather than what they can give. When I say give, I do not mean money necessarily. When it comes to giving it is the giving of yourself that really matters. I is the giving of yourself to increase the glory of God and to decrease whatever glory we may have in ourselves. In fact, if you back up a few verses to verse 27 John says this, "A person cannot receive even one thing unless it is given him from heaven" (John 3:27 ESV). So, with this being said, nothing we have or will ever have belongs to us. All of it belongs to God, and for God. So, when we seek self-fulfillment in the things that belong to God we are looking for the wrong things. Christianity is not self-fulfillment it's God fulfillment. All we do is to be done for the glory of God.

One thing that I need to address in this chapter although I hate to, but I have to... It needs to be heard. There has always been a plague in Christianity of what we call the "Prosperity Gospel." If you want to be honest that name could actually be replaced with this chapter, The "Self-fulfillment Gospel." There are even pastors and TV evangelist that will even claim the name a prosperity preacher. You probably know exactly what I am talking about. They will be on TV or on the radio telling you that you can give for your healing, you can give for your blessing, you can give for your miracle. They are not asking for your time or effort in ministry. They are asking for your money. This is scary and dangerous because not only does this Gospel promote self-fulfillment for that preacher, but it promotes self-fulfillment for the giver... Why? Because they are either giving out of obligation or they are giving because they want some type of blessing. They expect to see something out of their giving, and when someone gives expecting something back it's not out of the same heart. So even when it comes to our giving of tithes and offerings it does not need to be done for self-fulfillment. It needs to be done so that he can increase, and we can decrease. This is a very important aspect even when it comes to our giving.

Without making it a footnote I do want to say I believe in giving. Not just of your time and effort but also in tithes and offering. However, it needs to be done cheerfully not expecting anything back because ultimately it all belongs to God anyway. Blessings really do come to those who give not expecting back. It may not come in ways that you expected but they will come.

Now since I have that part out of the way let's look at Judas. Judas was one of the twelve disciples that walked with Jesus, talked with Jesus, and certainly discipled in his name. All four of the gospels explicitly name Judas as one of the disciples. Even though Judas was a disciple he ended up betraying Jesus, and Jesus predicted this betrayal at the Last Supper.

"When evening came, Jesus arrived with the Twelve. While they were reclining at the table eating, he said, "Truly I tell you, one of you will betray me—one who is eating with me." They were saddened, and one by one they said to him, "Surely you don't mean me?" "It is one of the Twelve," he replied, "one who dips bread into the bowl with me. The Son of Man will go just as it is written about him. But woe to that man who betrays the Son of Man! It would be better for him if he had not been born."
Mark 14:17-21 NIV

This claim by Jesus must have been a shocking moment for all twelve. I'm sure at this point even Judas was shocked not knowing yet what he may do. There is no real recorded motive as to why Judas betrayed Jesus. The only thing we do know is that he received a payment of thirty pieces of silver. This is our sign that Judas betrayed Jesus out of self-fulfillment. Anyone who would accept money over Jesus in any shape form or fashion is looking for self-fulfillment. This means to Judas the money and or what he could do with it had increased above God. The danger in this is anything we increase above God is idolatry. So what happens to Judas next?

"With the payment he received for his wickedness, Judas bought a field; there he fell headlong, his body burst open and all his intestines spilled out."
Acts 1:18 NIV

What happened to Judas seems to be a very horrific scene. Honestly it seems to be a horror movie. Did his body just explode? In the middle of the things he purchased with the money. He died in a way that was so bad the people of Jerusalem called his field the "Field of blood." Can you imagine your death being so bad they name your property after your death? The important point here is that self-fulfillment always ends up tragic. Not sometimes but all the time.

Self-Fulfillment always leads to Self-Destruction

Now coming back to the practical sense of things... The immediate collapse into death was not just for people like Judas, or Ananias and Sapphira. There is a spiritual death that has come upon the Church due to the seeking of self. Although Christianity is growing, and we have mega churches everywhere I do fear many are seeking personal pleasure. Some only go to Church for specific reasons like good music, good preaching, nice facility, my parents go there, my friends go there, they have nice programs for the kids, etc. etc... Rarely do you hear anymore I go because of Jesus and what he done for me. These are all articles of self-fulfillment. There is nothing wrong with enjoying these things (Lord knows I do). But we must be careful what our priorities are in the reasons we go and serve God. The question I have heard asked before is this... What if the music stopped? What if the preacher didn't preach the way YOU like? What if the fancy pyrotechnics were gone? Would you still go to church? Would you still serve him? These are questions we should ponder to seek the heart.

Self-fulfillment is also something that plagues the non-Christian as well. In fact, truth be told many who choose not to follow Christ are living their entire lives in a self-seeking manner somehow. The fact that Jesus asks us to give our entire lives to him in full devotion scares many away. This is not an easy task and at times it is not fun (as mentioned in a previous chapter), and it's not supposed to be. Self-fulfillment leaves us with momentary pleasures that will soon fade. But when we seek to fulfill Jesus and his great commission it gives eternal pleasures that no man can fathom.

Not only should we seek to increase God, but we should seek to increase each other. When Jesus was asked out of all the commandments (which were over 600 in the Old Testament) which is the great (best, or main) commandment. "Jesus replied: " 'Love the Lord your God with all your heart and with all your soul and with all your mind.' This is the first and greatest commandment, and the second is like it: 'Love your neighbor as yourself.'" (Matthew 22:37-39 NIV). Not only do we need to love God with everything inside of us. But just as we do, we should love each other, and in this love comes services. In this love comes a fulfillment for the needs of our neighbor. If we are constantly seeking to serve God and others there is no way we can be self-seeking.

There is nothing wrong with enjoying life and having nice things. We do have to be careful in not allowing "self" to get in the way of God. We can't allow our own personal desires to trump the desires of our Savior. So enjoy the music, enjoy the pyrotechnics, enjoy the preaching, and enjoy each other. But most of all enjoy God getting the glory in it all.

SECTION 2

WHAT BEING A CHRISTIAN

"IS"

CHAPTER 7

IS A GLASS HOUSE

"You are the light of the world. A city set on a hill cannot be hidden. Nor do people light a lamp and put it under a basket, but on a stand, and it gives light to all in the house. In the same way, let your light shine before others, so that they may see your good works and give glory to your Father who is in heaven."
Matthew 5:14-16 ESV

Being a Christian is a glass house. Being in a "glass house" can at times be the toughest part of Christianity. When I speak of a glass house, I am not referring to a literal home made of glass. That would be very expensive and way above my pay grade. Imagine how weird that would be anyway... I am talking about we are the center of all things. Not because we want to be but because that is what follows us. We are seen from all corners physically and spiritually. We can't hide from anything. Especially from God! Everyone sees all we say and do, and they are watching. It feels like we are in a glass house with the world tuned in 24/7 waiting and watching for our next mistake. Kind of like that "Big Brother" thing. Now that we live in a world driven by social media it is much worse. Some of which is indeed brought on ourselves by what we post and engage in. I've personally come to the conclusion that this isn't always a good thing. Yes, social media can be good, but it can be bad. Don't believe me... Just share who your favorite presidential candidate is, if you stand for or against certain movements, or even your theological views. If you have many friends or acquaintances you are sure to find yourself in a debate, argument, or being judged. In fact, it can be so bad I personally chose to close all my social media outlets down while writing this book.

Being in a glass house is one of the major reasons many people are ashamed to claim Christ as their Lord and Savior. They know the very instance they do so everything changes. What you do from that moment is viewed through a different lenses. This is a sad reality, but it is very true. I mean think about it... People are not really watching those who don't bear the cross. If someone doesn't claim to be a Christ follower, we have no reason to watch their every move. But the moment they bare the name (Jesus), the world and sometimes even other Christians begin to look on waiting to see if we can hold to the expectations. They know you are bound to say or do something wrong. Even a Christ follower has a hard time of not making a mistake. Those watching us don't have the patience either. The moment we mess up they are ready to tarnish our testimony forever.

We have nothing to hide

As Christians we are to be open an honest about all things. I mean, lying is a sin too. But, we need to learn to do so without "hanging out all the dirty laundry." Living my life in a glass house is something I have learned to adapt to quite well. In fact, since I know I am being watched sometimes I do silly stuff to make religious folk cringe. Not sinful stuff, but silly stuff. I love to have fun openly to show them they can watch but it's ok. When we are living to the best of our ability in the pursuit of Holiness, we are doing what God intended. We have nothing to hide because our mistakes are just that... Mistakes! In all this we must remember though the world is watching. This means our pursuit does need to be one that is holy and sanctified. When we mess, up we get up, and then we tell the world "watch this" as we continue our pursuit of God.

The difference between us and those watching is simple. Both of us are going to mess up and make mistakes throughout life. But, Christians know what to do and where to go with their mistakes. Those watching don't know. It's up to us to continuously show them by example. Church isn't full of hypocrites. Church is full of people that are in a glass house and you just so happen to know our dirt. We are in Church to take a bath and get clean from the dirt. All the while a watching world continues to roll around in the mud as a pig.

Now you see me now you don't

So, you can see what we have done. You have it stored away in the filing cabinet of your brain. You will never forget, nor do you want to forget. This is the irony of the world holding on to our past. The scars we have in the flesh may be there and be able to be seen as long as we are on this earth. But in the spiritual world our mistakes are no more. They can't be seen by us, or anyone else. God wipes that slate clean so that it can never be known again.

Without an overflowing of scripture, I will share a few things God does with your sin. He forgives you of your sin. He covers our sin. He washes them away. He forgets our sins. He casts them into the sea. He took them upon himself on the cross! All throughout scripture we see God's mercy, grace, and forgiveness concerning our sins. So, worrying about how others feel should be the least of our worries.

You may not ever stand justified before man, but you will forever be justified in the eyes of God! So, you stand firm in that glass house. Let the haters hate and maybe even do a dance just for the world to see! Get to the window baby and watch this!

I need to calm down and remember I am writing a book not a sermon... lol... But for real thought... Let them watch us. They are watching now and will be watching when we

70

are taken up into glory, and then they can take all those files they have on us to the grave. God has us, He is holding us, and He knows our heart.

Since we are being watched we must be careful to serve him not out of obligation but joy. We must always bear fruit. It is by bearing fruit that they will know we are his disciples. This means being watched is not a bad thing at all. I don't want this chapter to portray that. In fact, it is a GOOD thing. Some people will not know truth unless they see it in action. You are their visual hope at redemption and grace. Just as much as their are people watching you to see the bad, there are those watching you to see the good. These are truth seekers! They are reading you, and you may be the only Bible they ever read. Your lifestyle can lead others to the cross, just by being watched. This is why it's more so a good thing living in a glass house. Our glass house is our ministry. The world can watch to scold us or they can join us. The choice is theirs. But for each one that joins us Heaven rejoices, and we should too. Look on Look on!

In Matthew 5 we see Jesus give direct confirmation of this truth. He said we are a light, and not just any light but the light of the world. We are the light that is bright created for all to see. Jesus makes a great point in saying we don't light a lamp to hide it. Kind of pointless for the lamp to be lit at that point. It is lit so everyone can see... "You're lit", "That's lit"... As my teenagers would say. God created you with the intentions of you being visible and tangible to everyone. By doing so you are able to shine light to everyone whether they want the light on or not. Let it burn Let it burn! The twofold purpose is so they can see your good works and give God the glory who is in heaven.

So be salty and be lit! Your being seen is serving it's purpose. Service for the King for the whole world to see!

CHAPTER 8

IS CONSISTENCY

"And let us not grow weary of doing good, for in due season we will reap, if we do not give up."
Galatians 6:9 ESV

Being a Christian is consistency. A consistency that never quits... A consistency that never gives up... A consistency from the heart. Being a Christian is being consistent at being a Christian. Sounds quite self-explanatory right. I mean, we all know you can't be a Christian one minute and wake up a non-Christian the next. That's quite impossible. Those who do "leave the faith" never truly had that faith from the beginning. Hebrews 11 tells us that justifying faith is one that is sure, certain, absolute, and convicting. This doesn't mean we will not struggle with aspects of our faith because we certainly will. It does mean our saving faith is consistent. We believe and have faith no matter what the situation or storm. Doing good is part of our DNA and we never get tired of doing so. We are consistent in doing good, all good. There is no base standard here in the good we do, but it is that we are good in all we do. There is no greater feeling in life than the feeling of doing good. Especially when it is to someone else.

Sunday Morning Punch Card

Those who carry what I will call the Sunday morning punch card are NOT practicing consistency. These are those whom come to church every Sunday morning and Wednesday nights but that's it. You see their beautiful smile and their Sunday's best (nice clothes) once or twice a week and that's it. Have a fellowship or some sort of work day and they will never show. Special events they never show. I mean we are to overlook this because they pay their tithes right? Nah... It is our job whether someone is a giver or not to help disciple people into a life of consistency. Not those who clock in on Sunday morning at 10am just to clock out at 11:30am and that's it for them. No bible studying on their own or anything. That Sunday Jesus is literally all they get other than a possible Elevation worship song on the radio, or a bible verse someone posted on Facebook. Honestly, ask yourself what have we become to think this is all there is to this thing? Do we honestly think that's all God desires and deserves of our time?

I have a fun game for you to try... For those that are married it is called "marriage roulette." For those that are not married I have a game for you next be patient. Since church is normally one 2-3 times a week I want you to try something... I want you to pick 2 days a week to love your spouse. Or at least only show them love them 2 days. The rest of the week you need to not communicate with them or pay them any attention. For those that are not married you will play "employment roulette." I want you to pick 2 days a week you go to work, and only go on those days. Don't call in or pay your employer any attention on the other days. When they ask where you been just make up some lame excuse.

Disclaimer: If either of these games end up in a train wreck for your marriage or a lost job, I am not held responsible. In fact, I want to go ahead and let you know both relationships will be lost if you play these two games! So, I highly advise you DO NOT try this at home!

If consistency in marriage matters, consistency to your employer matters, consistency practicing your golf swing matters (in my case playing basketball), consistency in school matters, and all other things in life we practice consistency then wouldn't you think God deserves that same consistency... If you are inconsistent in your walk with God, there is a problem! He has no longer become a priority in your life and if God is not a priority do you even have a relationship with him? Anything and everything that get in between you and God is idolatry. Nothing more and nothing less. A lack of consistency with the creator of the universe (your loving and caring Heavenly Father) for any reason is idolatry. This does not mean all the things you do in life not pertaining to God are idolatry. But it does mean all the things in life you elevate above God are.

Salvation linked to Consistency

Without making this book to theological I do feel the need to address this issue so you can examine your heart. It is one of the areas in my walk that I have had to examine quite deeply.

My biggest fear is I feel people fail to realize the link between consistency and salvation. The Bible does not directly tie anything to salvation other than Grace and Faith ("For by grace you have been saved through faith. This is not your own doing; it is the gift of God, not a result of works, so that no one may boast." Ephesians 2:8-9 ESV). So, the giving of Grace from God and the response by Faith from you is the only thing that saves you. You can't do anything else! There are basically 2 main theological "camps" when it comes to maintaining this salvation. The first is that you can't lose it nor renounce it. The other is you can't lose it, but you can renounce it. Many people get caught up in wording by saying they believe you can or can't lose salvation and I believe the wording is incorrect because neither believe it can be lost. The more proper word would be renounced, or the more biblically correct term would be Apostasy.

Although these two groups of Christians differ in this area one thing I have noticed is they agree when it comes to consistency. Those that say a Christian can't renounce their salvation would say a lack of consistency and devotion to God would probably mean they were never saved from the start. Those who say Christians can renounce their salvation would say that lack of consistency could mean one is on the verge of renouncing their salvation by not making God priority. I'm not going to say which I think is the better view for I believe they are both needed and thought provoking when it comes to our walk. Neither groups say you are saved by what you do but yet whom you serve. Scripture is clear that you can't serve two masters. Also, the fruit of your labor will prove that you are his disciples.

For extra clarity I need to make note on this point that salvation is not determined by your church timecard. It is not determined on your event timecard. It is not determined on a consistency timecard. There will be many that do lots of things that are only consistent because it looks so impressive. Your salvation is based upon your Faith. Your Faith is the driving factor of your consistency. When we really have Faith in God, we live a life that speaks from the mountain tops "I can't get enough" because God is so so good. His grace is so amazing it naturally pushes us to not let anything waiver our walk with him. I'm not just going to serve him today, but I am going to serve him tomorrow. My service is my dedication through Faith.

Consistency though scripture

"Therefore, my dear brothers and sisters, stand firm. Let nothing move you. Always give yourselves fully to the work of the Lord, because you know that your labor in the Lord is not in vain."
1 Corinthians 15:58 NIV

"Commit to the Lord whatever you do, and he will establish your plans."
Proverbs 16:3 NIV

"And whatever you do, whether in word or deed, do it all in the name of the Lord Jesus, giving thanks to God the Father through him."
Colossians 3:17 NIV

There are many verses to apply here. Sometimes scripture needs no commentary. "Always give yourselves fully to the Lord", "Commit to the Lord", "Whatever you do" are all great indicators of a life of service and consistency. Here is one of my all time favorite passages in this context.

"Do you not know that in a race all the runners run, but only one gets the prize? Run in such a way as to get the prize. Everyone who competes in the games goes into strict training. They do it to get a crown that will not last, but we do it to get a crown that will last forever. Therefore I do not run like someone running aimlessly; I do not fight like a boxer beating the air. No, I strike a blow to my body and make it my slave so that after I have preached to others, I myself will not be disqualified for the prize."
1 Corinthians 9:24-27 NIV

I love this passage by Paul for so many reasons. The main reason is probably because I love sports and fitness and he ties all that greatness into this passage. Even boxing! I wonder who the Mike Tyson and Muhammad Ali was back then... Anyways... what Paul was doing here was exhorting the Corinthian Church into a life of consistency and devotion. When you are in competition of any sort you have to diligently practice, study, and work at being better for that competition. Our lives should be that we are running a race that we never want to stop running. We have a finish line ahead that's so far beyond comprehension. We have a prize unending.

Being a Christian of consistency doesn't necessarily mean being at every church service or event. But, it does mean when you are not you are reading, praying, and serving Him in all you do. We are in the midst of a pandemic called COVID-19 and many people are not going to church for many different reasons. Some justifiable and some not so much. I guess as a leader myself I want to make sure those who aren't and or can't are still in the training room getting ready for the boxing match. It is my prayer that they watch service online, pray, and read their Bibles. Leaders long to know their people are being consistent in this race. My heart as a leader is for you to read this and gain strength. It's to remind us that Christ really is who we live for. We live for nothing else but him. I pray that you can find consistency in your walk.

Servant don't stop serving... Don't lose heart... You are about to reap a harvest!

CHAPTER 9

IS DIVERSITY

"John said to him, "Teacher, we saw someone casting out demons in your name, and we tried to stop him, because he was not following us." But Jesus said, "Do not stop him, for no one who does a mighty work in my name will be able soon afterward to speak evil of me. For the one who is not against us is for us. For truly, I say to you, whoever gives you a cup of water to drink because you belong to Christ will by no means lose his reward."
Mark 9:38-41 ESV

B eing a Christian is diversity. Diverse in many different ways. I love the passage of scripture in Mark 9 when Jesus was being told that these "other people" were casting out demons in his name. In this narrative it's very clear that the disciples seen these other people as different than them. Probably having slightly different theological and doctrinal beliefs. However, what they were doing was in the name of Jesus Christ. So, it seems that although they had differences in theology and doctrine, Jesus was ok with what they were doing in his name. Not only was he OK with what they were doing, but he told the disciples not to stop them. Just because somebody is not technically with you does not mean they are against you.

Diversity among groups

In Christianity we have a plethora of denominations. In fact so many it can be taxing as to know who, what, when, and where. There are so many different denominations and non-denominations I don't know that we even have the number of them or that we even can. Some people have tried to use this as an excuse to not go to church or even serve Christ. They ask questions like "So many different views who is right?" and "Do they disagree with each other?"... There are tons of other questions this has raised towards our movement. But I want to ask you this question in contrast. Is this really a bad thing?

To me having so many choices of places to worship is indeed a good thing. God has provided us (all of us) with a place we can call home. We just have to search, and if you are fully committed you will not mind searching. In fact you will want to search and enjoy the journey in doing so. Because, you will meet some amazing loving people from all denominations and all walks of life. As far as who is right and who is wrong... Well there are probably areas where all of them are a little right and a little wrong. But, these are areas of less importance and many of which are personal preferences read into scripture, or even personal convictions. None of which are issues pertaining to salvation. In fact, if that group or church or denomination believes in salvation is by Grace through Faith ALONE... This it is a foundational truth that all Protestant Christians believe. So, whether you must wear a dress and suit, read hymns, or rock pyrotechnics are all secondary issues that don't matter at the end of the day.

"The reality is that different denominations tend to reach different kinds of people, and if you're going to reach all the people of the city, you're going to need all of the different denominations." - Timothy Keller (Facebook post)[6]

I love this truth by Timothy Keller. Do you know what he is saying? He is saying we have diversity and we need diversity. So, for people to say they don't go to church or serve God for this reason is indeed a cop-out. It is our job to find a place or group where the Gospel is preached without compromise, and to serve there with joy and gladness. Your city needs you and your ministry. You have the ability to reach people that others do not have. You can and will be used even thought your style is a little different. As long as the message is the same!

---

[6] https://www.facebook.com/TimKellerNYC/

Diversity among the people

Each church should either be a church of diversity or a church that welcomes diversity. By this, I mean ALL types of people. No one under any circumstances should ever feel like they can't go to a church. I don't care what it is... If they are a saint or sinner, they should be welcome. If they are black, white, or brown they should be welcome. If they are gay, straight, or both they should be welcome. If they are rich or poor, they should be welcome. If they are on drugs or clean they should be welcome. So not only do we have the great diversity among groups, but we have this great diversity among people. Now this does not mean we tickle ears! Let me say that again... This does NOT mean we are to compromise biblical truths for the sake of making people comfortable. Our job is to make people comfortable in a physical aspect not a spiritual aspect. If we are making them comfortable in their sin, then we are doing it all wrong. Likewise, if we are physically making them uncomfortable because of who they are we are doing it all wrong. There must be a balance.

God's promise of Diversity

We all know that God had a chosen people all throughout scripture. That was and still is the Jews. As many have made this complicated over the years it wasn't and isn't that they are special above anyone else. It is more so that

God used them throughout history in extravagant ways. God's promise is extended to all people to all nations.

"For I am not ashamed of the gospel, because it is the power of God that brings salvation to everyone who believes: first to the Jew, then to the Gentile."
Romans 1:16 NIV

Gentiles were all Greek or others that were not Jews. So, if you are reading this you are a Gentile in context and that means salvation is for you. This is EVERYONE! God doesn't have a specific chosen only formula. He is a God of diversity and extends saving Grace to all. He does not show partiality, and neither should we. As someone who has a Wesleyan leaning this rings even more throughout my spirit. I try my best to make all people feel loved and welcomed. If someone makes them feel uneasy let's let that someone be God and His Word. Not us!

God's promise of diversity is not just seen here. When John was able to look in and get a glimpse of heaven here is what he saw.

"After this I looked, and there before me was a great multitude that no one could count, from every nation, tribe, people and language, standing before the throne and before the Lamb. They were wearing white robes and were holding palm branches in their hands."
Revelation 7:9 NIV

Notice something amazing in this verse? They were all together! Not behind different walls or in different churches. No social media to argue on. No social distancing. No masks. Not separate denominations or groups. All together and all worshipping the same God. People from everywhere, every color, every language... I can't wait for that day! Being united with people and being united with God! Yes please!

Something I find interesting about this verse is how God specifically allowed John to see this. Instead of just people worshipping, John was able to distinguish characteristics of these people. God made sure of this and made sure it was recorded in scripture. I believe the purpose is for us to know now. Because, we live in a world where we know these things and sometimes allow them to divide. This is God's way of letting us look in with John and see that although there may be divisions and differences here on earth, there will be no such thing in heaven.

There is a place for you

The main point in me writing this chapter is to remind those whom are in the body of Christ already to be more longing and compassionate to everyone. That includes the church down the road that does things a little different. That includes that person that is living a lifestyle that is totally against God. You can be that person to reach them if you remember they too can be part of that vision John had.

It is for those whom read this and feel as if diversity may be one of the reasons you can't seem to find your groove in Christianity. I want to encourage you that our diversity is a good thing and not something to cause division. Those in Christianity that have allowed diversity to cause division need to examine their hearts. I want you to know there is a place for you! That place is full of imperfect people, from the pulpit to the parking lot. But, you do indeed belong. Jesus died for you... All of you!

CHAPTER 10

IS COMFORTING

"Blessed be the God and Father of our Lord Jesus Christ, the Father of mercies and God of all comfort, who comforts us in all our affliction, so that we may be able to comfort those who are in any affliction, with the comfort with which we ourselves are comforted by God."
2 Corinthians 1:3-4 ESV

Being a Christian is comforting. This is probably one of the greatest parts about being a Christian. We can live a life of blessed hope and comfort knowing the promises God has for his children. Now when I say being a Christian is comforting, I do not mean being a Christian is living a life of comfort here on earth. In fact, for many it can be the exact opposite. There are so many Christians living in horrible situations. But, the reason they are Christian is because their faith in what Jesus did for them, and the promises God has for those who follow him. We have comfort that goes way beyond the walls of this world.

One of my favorite sayings goes something like this, (I would rather live my entire life as a follower of Jesus Christ and die to find out it was not real, than to live my life not believing and die to find out it was real). Although, through Faith we are certain of our convictions about God. The saying rings true that whether true or not, we have nothing to lose. Because, we have nothing to lose we can rest at night knowing we are safe and secure.

A world of discomfort

We live in a world filled with absolute turmoil. Everywhere we turn there is division, hatred, racism, wars, fires, earthquakes, tornados, if you name it... It is indeed happening in this day we live. It seems no one can find comfort, or rest. The lack of joy and love seem to be the icing on the cake. Even many Christians are living with the disease of depression and anxiety. We are plagued with people walking away from the Faith. What in the world is happening? Can things get worse? What can we do?

The main issue is people are seeking comfort in the things of this world. People are even relying on people for their temporary comfort, and let me tell you... You will NOT find it in this world, nor should you be seeking comfort the world offers. Everything this world gives is temporary. Literally everything from friendships to relationships and even accomplishments are only satisfying for a short moment. All things in this life will eventually "drop the ball" on us leaving us uncomfortable. At some point in your life even people will fail you somehow. Remember we are all imperfect and trying to find eternal comfort in something or someone that is full of imperfections will eventually turn on you. You will have an ever-growing hole in your heart called "discomfort."

Jesus is our comfort

Our comfort is in Jesus... It's quite that simple. Not us, who we are, or what we do. Our comfort can't come from ourselves because we are flawed from birth. We are sinners that know no good. We can only find comfort in him whom provides comfort. Jesus told us he would send a Comforter.

> "And I will pray the Father, and he shall give you another Comforter, that he may abide with you for ever; Even the Spirit of truth; whom the world cannot receive, because it seeth him not, neither knoweth him: but ye know him; for he dwelleth with you, and shall be in you."
> John 14:16-17 KJV

We have a comforter in the Holy Spirit that is going to abide with us forever. Jesus did not tell us to seek comfort in anything. He told us He was sending us a Comforter. Some translations call Him the Advocate and others call Him the Helper. So it's comforting to know Jesus has sent his Holy Sprit to dwell inside of us. He is not only our Comforter, but our Advocate and Helper!

When we are faced with the troubles of this world, we have someone to turn to. Christians have direct access to God through the Holy Spirit sent by Jesus. We have no reason to live in worry, fear, or doubt. Even in the midst of our struggles we have God.

"Rejoice in the Lord always. I will say it again: Rejoice! Let your gentleness be evident to all. The Lord is near. Do not be anxious about anything, but in every situation, by prayer and petition, with thanksgiving, present your requests to God. And the peace of God, which transcends all understanding, will guard your hearts and your minds in Christ Jesus."
Philippians 4:4-7 NIV

Being a Christian is Comforting! We can rejoice and rejoice ALWAYS. That means in every situation, trial, temptation, and hardship. We don't have to walk in anxiety or depression. All we have to do is continuously seek God and he will give us peace. A peace that goes far beyond what the mind can understand. Not only can we not understand, but the world can't either. Those who do not know Jesus will look on wondering how we can still face this evil world with Joy.

Heaven is our home

Probably the most important reason we can live in comfort is knowing this simple truth. Heaven is indeed our home. This world we are current living is temporary. It's almost like one big dream that determines our eternity. We will all one day wake up and be in either

Heaven or Hell. Yes, there is a Heaven to gain and a Hell to shun. The alternative to eternity in God's presence is eternity outside of God's presence, and no one has ever experienced a second outside of God's eternal presence. Those who are born again into God will be in His presence for eternity. This is the ultimate hope of the born-again believer. This is why so many of us can walk right through this life with the attitude of "Oh well" as my Aunt Kathryn used to say. No matter what situation she was faced with in life it was always "Oh well." Christians need to have that attitude towards our trials because the Bible says all of this "mess" is only for the moment.

"For our light and momentary troubles are achieving for us an eternal glory that far outweighs them all. So we fix our eyes not on what is seen, but on what is unseen, since what is seen is temporary, but what is unseen is eternal."
2 Corinthians 4:17-18 NIV

So, our afflictions are "Oh well", because we know something better is on the horizon. It's an attitude of peace and comfort... It going to be ok! Not my promise but God's promise! It won't last long... It's only a short trial. As Christians we are not exempt for hardship. But in our hardship, we rejoice as it is our reminder of greater things to come. We celebrate the unseen eternal blessings that are coming our way. We are to give no attention to the seen temporary trials we face now.

Yes, there will be some tough days. Yes, you will face uncomfortable times. Yes, Yes, Yes... But the overall sum of your life and walk in Christ need to be one of Comfort. The battle you are facing and will face (because they are coming) is already won! Jesus did not just take your sins upon the cross. He took everything you face with him. Meaning no matter what you go through in this life Jesus went through it with much more punishment. My friend be at peace... Live with joy knowing you win! Our God is so good to us we can't even fathom his greatness.

Our hope is in Jesus

Our Joy is in Jesus

Our victory is in Jesus

Our COMFORT is in Jesus

CHAPTER 11

IS TOUGH LOVE

"Rather, speaking the truth in love, we are to grow up in every way into him who is the head, into Christ,"
Ephesians 4:15 ESV

"Sanctify them in the truth; your word is truth."
John 17:17 ESV

Being a Christian is tough love. The struggle of our walk goes to great depths when it comes to this. I will address love in a general sense in the last chapter of this book. Love being the basis of all we do, and part of that love is tough love. This is a love that does not compromise truths. Sometimes one of the hardest things we have to do is be truthful to people we love. Especially when it comes to things that are wrong or don't align with Godly morals. This in turn causes us to have to be tough towards everyone, and not just those we are close to. In fact, we need mentors and people around us that will keep that hard shell of tough love pressed against us to keep us straight in our walk.

As a young boy I lived in a small country town called Vanleer Tennessee. It was one of those towns where everyone knew everyone. I had friends all over that town that I would go see all the time. There were even a couple of them that practically lived with us. My parents were very cool about allowing me to spend lots and lots of times with friends growing up. The church of that town was Faith Baptist Church led by pastor Jerry and sister Sue Jenkins. They are still leading and pastoring in that town to this day! I loved church so much I used to walk to church just about every time the doors opened. I was the only one in my household that attended church. My parents always loved God and were believers, but they didn't attend church. I did and I loved it! I would go to the alter so many times and feel God's great grace and love wrapped around me so tightly. It was amazing... But like most of us I became a teenager. We moved to Hickman County Tennessee where I spend my middle school and high school years. This is when things changed for me. Teenage male hormones, drinking, drugs, fighting, you name it I was in it. I was influenced and spent most of my time with an older cousin that was going through deep trials in his life. He loved me but he also enabled me. I got to a point with drinking and smoking marijuana quite bad to the point I could not hide it anymore. I remember the night of my 16th birthday party when my dad intercepted some liquor we had hidden, before the party even started. He had a blow up with my cousin and they tightened down on me as parents. I will never forget the moment they looked at me and said, "We don't care if you get mad and hate us forever, but we are going to have to show you tough love." I really had no clue what tough love was at this age and didn't really care. I just thought they were being "jerks" for placing rules on me that kept me from having what I thought at the time was "fun." Fast forward ahead to now I know exactly what they meant by "tough love" and I thank God everyday for such a love as that. If it were not for that tough love I probably would not be where I am today. In fact there is no telling what direction my life would have headed. I am forever in debt to my wonderful parents for risking my anger towards them for the sake of my future.

As a father myself I now realize the depth and importance of tough love so much more. It hurts me so bad to ground or spank one of my daughters for doing wrong. This is what makes it so tough. What they don't understand at that age is why mom or dad punishes them like they do. They also don't understand the slight pain it gives them is magnified to us. We hurt worse than they do when we have to punish them. Can you imagine how God feels? He is our Heavenly Father that allows us to go through different trials and temptations knowing it brings us closer to him. Can you imagine the tough love Jesus experienced on the cross knowing the Father was allowing our punishment upon his Son? All the while we were crucifying Him, He asked his Father to "forgive us." My love for my children is the only reason I punish them. If I did not love them, I would allow them to stray in ways that could lead in to devastation and destruction.

Many of you reading this book have either fully faced tough love and have a full grasp of it's splendor, have faced it and didn't realize what it is, or you have not yet faced it in a practical sense. Whatever your case maybe I want to try and briefly show why it is a part of our walk, and why it is absolutely necessary. Even though it can be hard to understand and a hard "pill to swallow." But I swallowed it on so can you.

The scripture tells us to share "truth in love." If I were to rephrase that for you it would say "be tough in love." The word truth in the passage is the tough part. Sometimes people just don't want to hear the truth. The truth hurts and hurts bad sometimes. Like in my instance the truth was I needed to stop having what I thought to be fun because it was not getting me anywhere. In my mind that was hog wash because I could control what I was doing and at the drop of a hat be successful. Or it could have been that I was still home under my parents, wings and didn't realize the task of growing up and being on my own. As Christians the truth part is indeed the tough part. The truth is the morals, standards, and ways of living that God has set. It's not our truth that we are sharing it is his. Our responsibility is to share that truth without compromising, and in the same breath be loving. How is this possible? How can we be loving and share a contrary view with someone knowing it will hurt them or make them mad? The answer... Love

Loving someone with true love has and will always mean being truthful to them. For one you don't lie to people you love, and second your truth is to help them. Even when they don't like it. For instance, we hear the "judge not" scripture bomb used so much as I mentioned in a previous chapter. The issue with that is many times people mistake us sharing the truth as being judgmental. We are not being judgmental we are being loving. Now yes there are those that are being judgmental and not trying to help. But I am referring to those that tell you the truth in a loving fashion... By the way the context of that passage actually tells us to judge but do so with a righteous judgement. Meaning to make sure we are clean of the same thing we are judging.

Sharing truth can be one of the toughest things we are to do as Christians. Especially when the world can be leery of our biblical truths. There have been so many Christians share truth with a hateful evil judgmental attitude that it makes is tough for us trying to share it with love. I have many friends that struggle with sinful lifestyles that I love dearly. Everything from LGBT, to drugs, to alcohol, to sex, you name it I have friends and family evolved in it all. Our approach to these people is very important to keeping them close, and having them close is the only way we can guide them to truth. When I say close, I don't mean a closeness that causes us to fall, but a closeness that lets them know we do love them although we disagree. Jesus was our prime example of such lifestyle.

"Once again Jesus went out beside the lake. A large crowd came to him, and he began to teach them. As he walked along, he saw Levi son of Alphaeus sitting at the tax collector's booth. "Follow me," Jesus told him, and Levi got up and followed him. While Jesus was having dinner at Levi's house, many tax collectors and sinners were eating with him and his disciples, for there were many who followed him. When the teachers of the law who were Pharisees saw him eating with the sinners and tax collectors, they asked his disciples: "Why does he eat with tax collectors and sinners?" On hearing this, Jesus said to them, "It is not the healthy who need a doctor, but the sick. I have not come to call the righteous, but sinners."
Mark 2:13-17 NIV

So, Jesus has to deal with the wonderful accusation of being a friend of sinners. Everyone looked on questioning his reason. When you read this do you honestly think Jesus was hanging with these people compromising the Word of God? Absolutely not! In fact, he was showing them truth in love. In fact, Jesus many times in his ministry actually showed truth by loving. I tell people all the time that sometimes my best ministry has come through just loving others without all the religious activity (whatever that is). Just the presence of Jesus with those sinners made all the difference in the world. The very reason Jesus was here was to set sinners free and that would not have been possible without loving them with truth.

As you continue your walk with the Lord always be truthful and loving at the same time. They go together like biscuits and gravy, like steak and baked potato, and now I am hungry. We don't compromise God's word to be loving. We live God's word in truth to be loving. Smile more, laugh more, live more, be more, and love more.

Don't forget... Be tough in doing so!

CHAPTER 12

IS LOVE

""For God so loved the world, that he gave his only Son, that whoever believes in him should not perish but have eternal life." John 3:16 ESV

B eing a Christian is love. Because love is the foundation of our faith and love is who God is. Christianity as a whole was founded on love. In John 3:16 the Bible says "for God so loved the world." This is the foundation for who God is and what God does. Love is the essence of all things in life even if you're not a Christian. I have never met anyone that does not want to be loved. Without love God is not God and Christianity does not exist. Other people and religions do love, but that love is not the same love. Our love is not still buried in a tomb. Our love was raised on the third day and lives. Our love not only lives but he lives in us. I was able to skim the surface on "tough love" in the previous chapter. In this chapter I hope to hit love in a little deeper meaning. I want the idea of God's love and our response to radiate in your heart and mind. When you sit this book down, I want you to be able to look up and smile knowing you are loved.

God is love

In John 3:16 we see a breakdown of God's love. God's love for the world is so real and so deep that he sent his son (his only son) to die on a cross FOR us. The depths of this is mind blowing and sometimes hard to fathom. What have we done to deserved such great love? As humans we are in constant war with God through our sinful nature. Romans 3:23 says all of us have sinned against God. Sinning against the Sovereign creator of the universe is not smart. It's kind of like walking up to the biggest baddest strongest human on earth and slapping them in the face. Except it can't even be compared to that because God is much stronger and Sovereign than our small brains can imagine. So, we have all rebelled against God... ok... You get the point. We do not deserve his love at all. But he loves us anyway.

My favorite story (other than the redemption story of Jesus) in the Bible pertaining to God's love is the fall of Adam and Eve. When God placed Adam in the garden, He gave him one simple rule.

"And the Lord God commanded the man, saying, "You may surely eat of every tree of the garden, but of the tree of the knowledge of good and evil you shall not eat, for in the day that you eat of it you shall surely die."
Genesis 2:16-17 ESV

God told him you can eat from every tree in the garden. I am sure there were tons and tons of beautiful fruitful luscious trees in the garden. But of all these trees there is only one you can't eat from. That is the tree of knowledge. It was a simple rule for Adam to follow. I mean if I were at a vineyard and had tons of vines I could choose from and was told to leave one of the vines alone I don't think it would be an issue. Unless of course I was tricked as they were. The enemy is definitely tricky.

What God says next is what blows my mind and expresses God's love for humanity from the very first human beings to walk this earth. He says "for in the day you eat of it you shall surely die." In others words if you don't follow this one simple rule that I (GOD) gave you, I will take away the very breath I gave you! You will no longer live because you don't deserve life. On that day and in that moment, you will be no more. What does God need with us anyway? Especially if we are not going to follow one simple rule. Instant death is indeed what Adam and Eve both asked for and it is what they deserved. But what actually happened when they ate from the tree?

When you are reading this in Genesis 2 and come to Genesis 3, when they eat from this tree you can feel immediate tension. It's like a drum roll is taking place in scripture and there is fixing to be this huge annihilation take place. It feels as if your bible is about to just take off flying through the room or something. I mean come on Adam... You were just told what was going to happen in the previous chapter and you are already disobeying the

God that created you and Eve. Bro what is wrong with you?

So, they ate from the tree and then God destroys them... No! He does not destroy them. He gives them the sense to know they have messed up. They realize they are unclothed and begin trying to hide from God... Sounds like many people today doesn't it. They make a mistake and act as if it can be hidden from God... Yeah right! Instead of taking their life he lets them live. He places a punishment on them that will plague humanity forever, and this punishment isn't because he is mean. It is a reminder to them and to us of his love. Because instead of him taking our very breath from us when we rebel against him... He provides us with more life to live and experience his grace, love, and mercy. That's what our trials in life are to remind us. Not of his wrath or anger but of his love. Even when we sin our loving God allows us to live... We don't deserve life but he lets us live.

This is just one of many stories of God's love for us. There has been entire books and volumes written about God's love for us. This is one of my favorite stories of God's love. The entire bible is a book of his redemptive love for us all. It all reaches its climax in the story of Jesus Christ. God's love is real, it's deep, it's eternal, and most of all it's sacrificial. Even as I write this I sit in amazement as I am reminded of his mercy and grace in my life. As you read in a previous chapter I had a time where I was in complete rebellion. But he loved me! Thank you, God, for your love.

God's love and free will

One of the things you hear that tries to contradict God's love is the "why calamity" question. I have heard this so much in my ministry and it has become a foundation for many apologist around the world.

"God created things which had free will. That means creatures which can go either wrong or right. Some people think they can imagine a creature which was free but had no possibility of going wrong; I cannot. If a thing is free to be good it is also free to be bad. And free will is what has made evil possible. Why, then, did God give them free will? Because free will, though it makes evil possible, is also the only thing that makes possible any love or goodness or joy worth having. A world of automata—of creatures that worked like machines—would hardly be worth creating. The happiness which God designs for His higher creatures is the happiness of being freely, voluntarily united to Him and to each other in an ecstasy of love and delight compared with which the most rapturous love between a man and a woman on this earth is mere milk and water. And for that they must be free."[7]
- C.S. Lewis

The overall reality of God's love is shown through free will. Which means we can do right or wrong. This is also the reason good and bad happen to all people whether they are Christian or not. Could God completely stop all

---

[7] https://www.cslewisinstitute.org/webfm_send/97

calamity? Absolutely! But in doing so he would be removing the very thing that shows his love toward us.

Imagine it this way. If you are in a relationship or marriage and if not imagine a best friend or even a parent. Would you rather, (A) You determine the thoughts and actions of your spouse or partner. In a way which you were able to control their love and actions towards you by making them love you. Or (B) Them freely choosing to love you and act in a loving manner towards you because they freely choose to. This action is not forced and happens solely because that person wants to under their own unforced will.

I am in total assumption that most would choose option (B). It is the essence of love for someone to freely love without being forced to do so. With this there is the option of evil. People can freely choose to rebel against God without being forced. But the ability to have this option is God's supreme love being displayed to us by our free choices.

Responding to God's love

> "We love because he first loved us."
> 1 John 4:19 ESV

As we have learned God loves us, and because of this love it demands a response from us. That response is love as well. We are to radiate love back to God and to others as well. His first love towards us is the only reason we are able to love back. Because of God's love to us first it is the supplier of our love to others. We are to love all people, no matter who they are, what they have done, or where they are from. Remember of all the commandments it was love God and love your neighbor. Everything rests on love! I love the passage in 1 Corinthians 12 that mentions all these gifts the Holy Spirit can give us. How important they are to the body of Christ. They help enable us in our ministry and they help enable others as well. But then you hit chapter 13.

> "If I speak in the tongues of men and of angels, but have not love, I am a noisy gong or a clanging cymbal. And if I have prophetic powers, and understand all mysteries and all knowledge, and if I have all faith, so as to remove mountains, but have not love, I am nothing. If I give away all I have, and if I deliver up my body to be burned, but have not love, I gain nothing."
> 1 Corinthians 13:1-3 ESV

We can be the most gifted human being on earth but without love we are absolutely nothing. No matter our gifts or services to God... If not done in love for love by love it is nothing. I have met some of the most gifted men and women in the world, but they had and attitude of a Tasmanian devil. Everything they did was for self and not out of love. These people scare the daylights out of me to be honest. When someone truly loves others, you can tell. Likewise when they don't, you can tell.

So, our response to God's love is simple. We need to love each other. Being a Christian is love to all of humanity good and evil. Out of all the chapters in this book this one is most important. When we love God and love others all of the rest will naturally fall into place.

My hopes are that by reading this you will be prompted into a deeper love of God and others. I know sometimes it's hard and we fail big time. Especially when people do us wrong. But we are to forgive as Christ forgave us. Love really does win and it is the pinnacle of our victory.

> ""This is my commandment, that you love one another as I have loved you."
> John 15:12 ESV

I LOVE YOU!

INTERESTING FACTS ABOUT THIS BOOK

1. It was written in the craziest year I have ever seen in my life. (2020)

2. It came to me as I seen so much division on social media.

3. It was not planned but pinned on me by God immediately while I was debating on Facebook.

4. It made me close all social media accounts down for a period of dedication to the book and to God.

5. Although not overly extensive I typed this entire book up in less than 1 month.

6. I was able to complete the book before some were able to get me endorsements for the book.

7. I had and still have no clue about proper "book writing skills."

8. I had zero help on the content other than God and study.

9. Probably 95% of this book was typed on my iPhone 6s Plus. The other 5% was typed on my iPad Pro.

10. I am a huge fan of the Bible in multiple translations. So choosing to use the ones I did was the hardest part of this book.

11. I lost sleep over this book.

12. I wanted everyone I know to write an endorsement (although not possible). Not to boost me but because I truly love them all.

13. I had much more in mind but wanted this book to match my personal attention span for books.

14. Being a Christian is love is and should be the longest chapter of this book and of your life.

15. I may have spent more time correcting my English errors than writing the book. #countryboystruggles

ABOUT THE AUTHOR

Casey Allen Fleet is the Youth and Media Pastor for Impact Student Miniseries at Higher Ground Church in Ahoskie, NC. He is Licensed and Ordained in the International Pentecostal Holiness Church. He has an Associate's Degree from Holmes Bible College. He was also a proofreader for the Modern English Version of the Bible. He is also a Bible reviewer for Bible publishers with an active YouTube. He is a loving Father of two beautiful daughters Allenah and Kenli Fleet. He is the husband of his amazing wife Heather Fleet. Lastly he loves to have fun and make people laugh. He can be "cray cray" at times in a good way. Just ask those around him!

DEDICATION

This book is dedicated to my beautiful daughters.

Allenah Grace Fleet and Kenli Hope Fleet...

I love you!

SUBSCRIBE TO MY YOUTUBE

HTTPS://WWW.YOUTUBE.COM/CHANNEL/
UC6XOUNGHAQ-576LWX8V1CSG

CASEY FLEET

Made in the USA
Columbia, SC
18 July 2022

63666387R00068